Sky High
published in 2008 by
Hardie Grant Egmont
Ground Floor, Building 1, 658 Church Street
Richmond, Victoria 3121, Australia
www.hardiegrantegmont.com.au

PEFC
PEFC/21-31-16

The pages of this book are printed on paper derived
from forests promoting sustainable management.

A CiP record for this title is available from the National Library of Australia

Text, illustration and design copyright © 2008 Hardie Grant Egmont

Cover and illustrations by Andy Hook
Based on original illustration and design by Ash Oswald
Typeset by Kirby Jones

Printed in Australia by McPherson's Printing Group

10

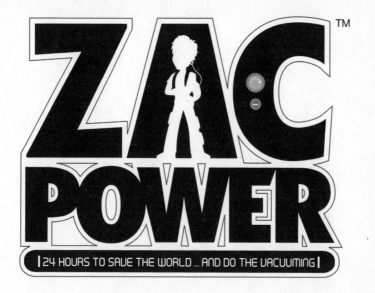

ZAC POWER ™

[24 HOURS TO SAVE THE WORLD ... AND DO THE VACUUMING]

SKY HIGH

BY H. I. LARRY

ILLUSTRATIONS BY ANDY HOOK

hardie grant EGMONT

CHAPTER... ...ONE

CRACK!

The eight ball zoomed across the table and dropped neatly into the corner pocket.

'That's the game, Agent Rock Star!'

Zac Power sighed. His older brother, Leon, had just beaten him at pool. Again.

'You got lucky,' said Zac grumpily, tossing his pool cue down onto the table.

'Six times in a row?' said Leon. 'I don't think so.'

'But you never miss!' Zac snapped. 'How is that even possible?'

'It's all simple geometry, Zac,' said Leon smugly, reaching down to pick up a ball. 'Oh, and a bit of physics, of course.'

'Of course,' said Zac sarcastically. He thought privately that being the world's biggest nerd gave his brother an unfair advantage at this game.

Zac was a top spy at an elite agency known as the Government Investigation Bureau. Leon also worked for GIB, but he was a technical officer in charge of creating gadgets and organising missions.

Which means I'm still much cooler than he is, Zac reminded himself.

'Another game?' Leon asked, racking up the balls. 'Best seven out of thirteen? Tell you what, you beat me this time and I'll do all that vacuuming mum asked you to do.'

'Fine,' said Zac. 'With a *normal* vacuum cleaner, though. No taking the easy way out with *that* thing.'

Zac pointed across the room to where a shiny purple gadget was sitting. The VacuuTron 5000. Leon had created it to cut down on cleaning time, and even Zac had to admit that it was a pretty cool invention.

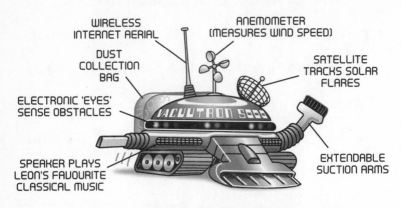

WIRELESS INTERNET AERIAL

ANEMOMETER (MEASURES WIND SPEED)

DUST COLLECTION BAG

SATELLITE TRACKS SOLAR FLARES

ELECTRONIC 'EYES' SENSE OBSTACLES

SPEAKER PLAYS LEON'S FAVOURITE CLASSICAL MUSIC

EXTENDABLE SUCTION ARMS

VACUUTRON 5000

If Leon's doing my chores, thought Zac, *he's going to do them the hard way.*

'OK,' said Leon. 'Deal. I'll even let you –'

But at that moment something started beeping in Leon's back pocket. He reached into his pocket and pulled out a small electronic gadget.

The device looked a bit like a video game console, but Zac knew it was so much more than that. It was a SpyPad, every GIB agent's most useful tool. A video phone, a magnet generator, a laser, and a hundred other gadgets all in one.

Right now, a woman's face was staring impatiently back at them from the screen.

'Agent Shadow,' said Leon, straightening up. 'What's the word?'

'I've just got the green light from Headquarters,' said Agent Shadow. 'We've finally got enough intel to launch Operation Bug Eye.'

'Leon,' Zac began, 'what's —'

'About time!' said Leon, cutting Zac off. 'I've had the gear ready for almost a week!'

'Of course you have,' said the other agent, rolling her eyes. 'But we needed to wait for confirmation from WorldEye. Is Agent Rock Star up to the challenge?'

'Yup,' said Leon, glancing across at Zac. 'As long as there's no pool-playing involved.'

'Sorry?' said Agent Shadow, confused.

'Noth – *ouch!*' said Leon, as Zac kicked him in the shin. 'Nothing.'

'Very well,' said Agent Shadow. 'I'll leave you to brief him.'

'Great,' said Leon. 'See you.'

The image of Shadow flickered out.

'What was all that about?' Zac asked.

'Just finalising the preparations for your next mission,' said Leon happily.

'Preparations?'

Leon sighed. 'Your missions don't just organise themselves, you know. We're hard at work for weeks before you even get one of these,' he said, dropping a little silver mission disk onto Zac's palm. 'You're just not usually around to see it.'

'Oh,' said Zac. He'd never really thought about what went on behind the scenes at GIB. 'So what's this mission you've all been working so hard on?'

'How does firing a high-powered rocket

into an invisible target sound?' said Leon.

'Piece of cake,' said Zac.

'Great!' said Leon. 'Did I mention *you're* the rocket?'

CHAPTER... ...TWO

Ten minutes later, Zac was speeding down the highway in Leon's Mobile Technology Lab.

The MTL was a secret laboratory on wheels that was currently disguised as a furniture removal van.

Zac pulled out his SpyPad and slipped the silver mission disk inside.

CLASSIFIED

An item of top-secret GIB technology has fallen into the hands of Professor Arthur Voler, a known enemy of the agency.

GIB has determined that Voler plans to use this stolen technology to break into GIB's high-security vault in Bladesville at 09:00am tomorrow.

YOUR MISSION

- Infiltrate Professor Voler's hide-out.

- Prevent Voler from breaking into the GIB vault.

- Retrieve the stolen technology.

- Detain Voler until he can be placed under arrest.

MISSION TIME REMAINING: 24 HOURS

END

Zac turned to Leon, who was standing at a workbench, tinkering with something that looked like a big metal backpack.

'Who is this Professor Voler guy?' he asked. 'I've never heard of him before.'

'Yeah, he's really secretive,' said Leon, without looking up. 'To be honest, we don't really know much about him. We don't even have a photo of him on –'

KA-BLAM!

Something exploded in front of Leon.

'What was that?' Zac shouted, ducking.

'Nothing!' said Leon quickly. 'Um, just running a final equipment check. Don't worry, I'm sure it won't do that when you're wearing it.'

'When I'm *wearing* it?'

'What we do know about Professor Voler,' Leon went on, eager to change the subject, 'is that he's the most cunning thief GIB has ever come across. He travels the world, stealing rare objects and classified technology for his private collection. He's snatched stuff from BIG, from Dr Drastic, from a bunch of museums…'

'And now he's stolen something from us,' Zac finished.

'Right,' said Leon, pulling a little jar from his pocket, emptying it into his hand, and turning to Zac. 'Nine days ago, Voler got hold of a top-secret GIB prototype as it was being transferred to Headquarters from our research facility in Silicone Valley.'

'A prototype for what?' asked Zac.

'This!' said Leon dramatically, thrusting out his hand.

Zac stared down at Leon's hand. There was nothing in it. He raised an eyebrow. 'Professor Voler is stealing our air?'

Leon shot Zac a don't-be-stupid look and said, 'Scan it.'

Zac set his SpyPad to Magnify and pointed it at his brother's hand. The SpyPad locked onto a tiny spot on Leon's palm and zoomed in. There was something there after all.

Hovering just above Leon's magnified

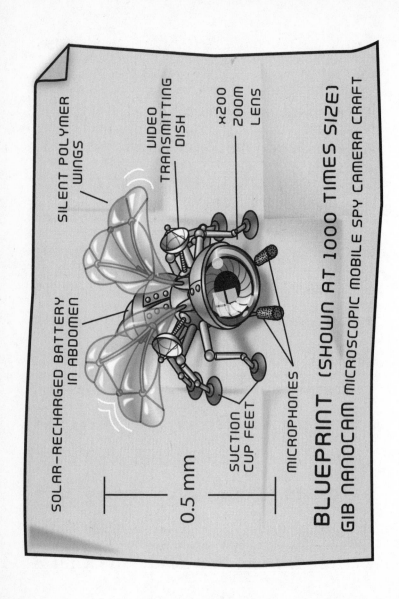

SOLAR-RECHARGED BATTERY
IN ABDOMEN

SILENT POLYMER
WINGS

VIDEO
TRANSMITTING
DISH

x200
ZOOM
LENS

0.5 mm

SUCTION
CUP FEET

MICROPHONES

BLUEPRINT (SHOWN AT 1000 TIMES SIZE)
GIB NANOCAM MICROSCOPIC MOBILE SPY CAMERA CRAFT

hand, tiny wings fluttering, was what looked like a one-eyed insect, except that it was made out of metal.

'Oh,' said Zac. 'What is it?'

'This,' said Leon proudly, 'is a NanoCam, the latest in GIB surveillance technology. Tiny, remote-controlled spy cameras, invisible to the naked eye. They're incredibly fast, and because they're so small, we can send them –'

'Pretty much anywhere,' said Zac.

'Exactly,' said Leon. 'The down side is that they're incredibly expensive to produce. Right now, this is one of only two in the world. Professor Voler has the other one, and we need you to get it back.'

'And where does the exploding backpack come into all of this?' Zac asked, looking sideways at Leon's workbench.

'Well,' said Leon, 'Voler likes to move around a lot, so he lives in the sky. His hide-out is an enormous jet plane, a bit like GIB's Hercules Transport.'

'So I'm going to fly up to him using the jetpack,' said Zac. 'Sounds simple enough.'

'Not quite,' said Leon. 'See, Voler has just outfitted his jet with some cloaking technology that he stole from BIG.'

'Wonderful,' said Zac. 'So that would be the invisible target you were talking about before?'

'Bingo,' said Leon. 'The good news is that the cloak was never meant to be used on anything as big as Voler's jet, so it's started to malfunction. We've caught a few glimpses of him making his way to Bladesville. It's not much, but it's enough to plot a course and get you aboard.'

'Assuming I don't explode on the way there,' muttered Zac.

CHAPTER...
...THREE

The Mobile Technology Lab pulled to a halt and Zac jumped out. Leon was right behind him, rolling the jetpack along the ground on a set of wheels. Enormous cornfields rose up on either side of the dirt road where they had stopped.

'Where are we?' Zac asked, looking around.

But Leon was busy tapping at his SpyPad.

'Quick,' he said, suddenly dashing off into the cornfield. 'This way!'

Zac followed, darting in and out of the rows of corn. Green leaves lashed at his face.

He might have been much faster than Leon in a fair race, but here Zac had the disadvantage of not having a clue where he was going. He almost lost track of his brother a few times.

'OK, we're here,' said Leon, stopping as suddenly as he had started.

Caught off-guard, Zac lurched forward and almost bowled his brother over.

'Voler's jet will be passing over in a couple of minutes,' Leon said, still trying to catch his breath. 'We'll need to time your launch exactly for this to work. Here, put this on.'

Leon rolled the jetpack over and Zac lifted it onto his back, staggering under the weight of it.

'Sorry it's so heavy,' said Leon, looking at his SpyPad. 'I needed to really cram in the fuel to get you up there.'

'It's fine,' said Zac firmly, straightening up.

'As it is, there's only enough fuel for a one-way trip. You'll also need *this* to get you back down to earth,' Leon added, handing Zac a pocket-sized fabric package marked MICRO-CHUTE.

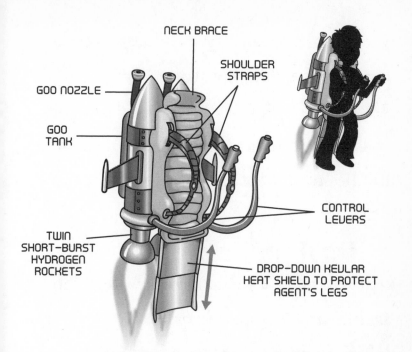

NECK BRACE

SHOULDER
STRAPS

GOO NOZZLE

GOO
TANK

CONTROL
LEVERS

TWIN
SHORT-BURST
HYDROGEN
ROCKETS

DROP-DOWN KEVLAR
HEAT SHIELD TO PROTECT
AGENT'S LEGS

GIB SHORT FLIGHT PERSONAL JETPACK

'Right,' said Zac, pocketing the
parachute and turning his attention back
to the jetpack.

He grabbed hold of the two handles
which now stretched out in front of him.

Each one had a small, round button on the top. 'So, how does this work?'

'Hold down the right-hand button to activate the jets,' said Leon. 'Tilt the handles to steer.'

'And to stop?'

'There's a proximity sensor in the pack that will beep as you approach Voler's jet,' said Leon. 'As soon as you hear it, hit the left-hand button and brace for impact.'

'No worries,' said Zac confidently.

'Oh, that reminds me,' said Leon, pulling a fluffy little square of black cloth from his back pocket. 'Here, take this.'

'Huh?' said Zac. 'What do I need a tiny towel for?'

'It's a super-absorbent polymer I've been working on,' said Leon. 'It compresses water particles to a fraction of their usual size, so it can soak up around twenty times as much liquid as a normal kitchen sponge. It'll come in handy, trust me.'

'Uh-huh,' Zac said as he tucked the towel into his jeans.

'Seventy-two seconds to launch,' said Leon, eyes back on his SpyPad.

Zac glanced at his watch.

Leon paused, and then cleared his throat loudly. 'There is one other little catch that I might not have mentioned.'

'You mean besides the fact that this jetpack could blow me to bits at any moment?' said Zac.

'Yeah,' said Leon. 'Here's the thing. Because Voler's jet is so high up, you'll need to really gun the jetpack to reach him. You'll be travelling at seriously high speed, too fast to pull out if something goes wrong. Either you hit the jet on your first try, or…'

'Or *what?*' Zac demanded.

'Or you keep going and burn up when you hit the earth's atmosphere,'

Leon finished grimly.

'Great,' Zac said. 'So, no pressure then.'

CHAPTER... ...FOUR

'OK, 30 seconds,' said Leon, glancing down at his SpyPad again. 'Remember, right button to activate, then wait for the beep and –'

'Yeah,' said Zac, gritting his teeth. 'Got it.'

'Got to run,' said Leon, turning around. 'Need to get clear of the blast radius. 20 seconds!'

And with that, Leon sprinted away through the cornfield.

Zac continued the countdown in his head. His white-knuckled hands gripped the jetpack controls. Only a few seconds left now.

Three...

Two...

One...

KA-BLAM!

It felt like the whole world exploded underneath Zac as he was catapulted skywards.

Looking down, Zac saw Leon staring up at him from the edge of a huge circle of charred-black earth — that take-off had burnt out almost half the cornfield!

Zac rocketed upwards. He kept his thumb down on the ignition and within seconds, the whole countryside was far beneath him.

Zac looked up, trying to catch a glimpse of the jet somewhere above him. But his eyes were watering from the wind rushing past his face, and he could barely see a thing.

Not that you'd be able to see a cloaked jet anyway, he reminded himself.

Zac had never travelled so fast in his life!

His fingers tensed on the handles as he tried to keep his path as straight as possible, doing his best to ignore the way the jetpack rattled and shook.

Zac could see an enormous white cloud up ahead, and before he knew it, he'd flown straight into it. He had just enough time to get soaked from head to toe by the water vapour before he burst out of the top of the cloud, still surging towards his invisible target.

BEEP

Already? Zac thought to himself, as the proximity sensor sounded. Apart from the fact that he half-expected to get smashed to bits against the underside of Voler's jet, this was actually pretty fun!

BEEP-BEEP-BEEP

Zac released his hold on the ignition and slammed down on the left button.

KER-SPLAT!

A stream of sticky yellow goo shot suddenly from the top of Zac's jetpack, covering him from head to toe.

What the —

SMACK!

Zac collided with something huge and solid in the middle of the air, and stuck fast.

Despite being completely grossed out, Zac had to admire his brother's invention.

The gel from the jetpack was obviously some kind of high-tech padding. It had softened Zac's impact like an airbag, so he wasn't splattered across the hull of the jet.

Not to mention sticking him fast so that he wouldn't fall straight back down to earth.

It was one of the most bizarre experiences Zac had ever had. There he was, flying upside-down through the air, glued to an invisible jet. And he looked as though he had just been sneezed on by a family of elephants.

Zac's eyes flashed to his watch.

Time to get inside. Pulling a sticky hand out of the goo, Zac felt his way around the surface of the jet until his fingers brushed past a large metal handle. He pulled on it and the door swung open with a click. Zac had to duck out of the way as several old-looking bags and boxes spilled out and went tumbling down to earth.

Must be the cargo hold, thought Zac.

Fighting against the gross slime that was still holding him to the underside of the jet, Zac slowly pulled himself up inside. He slammed the door shut behind him and stood up in the dark room.

Well, thought Zac, trying to flick the goo off his body, *I guess this explains the towel.*

He pulled the little black square out of his pocket and wiped himself down.

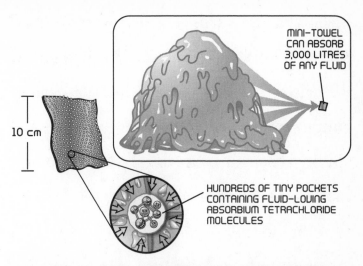

GIB ULTRA-ABSORBENT MINI-TOWEL

Amazingly, the tiny towel soaked up every last drop of goo from his body without being squeezed out once.

Zac switched his SpyPad to Torch and shone it around the room.

At first it looked like there was no way out of the cargo hold, but then Zac pointed his SpyPad upwards and saw a small, round hatch set into the ceiling. He reached up and unscrewed the hatch, revealing a narrow tunnel with a ladder leading up one side. Pulling himself onto the first rung of the ladder, Zac clambered up into the interior of the jet.

At the end of the tunnel was another hatch, which creaked noisily as Zac twisted it open. He stuck his head up through the hatch and looked around.

Zac blinked as his eyes adjusted to the light. He had been expecting to find a high-tech computer room or a laboratory filled with bubbling chemicals.

Instead, he had just emerged into a grand

lounge room filled with beautiful antique furniture. The walls were hung with paintings and lined with shelves crammed full of trophies, trinkets and gadgets.

It looked like the kind of place that might be owned by a really rich guy in an old movie.

Suddenly, a voice broke the silence, making Zac jump.

'Ah, Zachary Power!' it said. 'Do come in. I've been expecting you.'

CHAPTER... FIVE

Zac leapt out of the tunnel and whirled around. Smiling back at him from behind an ornate wooden table was a wrinkly old man. He was dressed in an expensive-looking suit and must have been at least 70 years old.

'Professor Voler?' said Zac uncertainly, wondering for a moment whether he'd boarded the wrong jet.

The old man nodded, and then gestured towards a large plasma screen on the wall.

Zac looked up at the screen and was startled to see an image of *himself* staring back. Zac raised his right hand. The Zac on the screen copied him exactly.

It was a live recording, coming from…

'That's right,' said Voler, as though reading Zac's mind. 'I've been using that marvellous NanoCam of yours to keep an eye on you. It's been buzzing around your ear for the last little while, transmitting video back to this screen.'

Zac could have kicked himself. Of course Voler had been expecting him!

He'd probably been tailing Zac with the NanoCam since he blasted off from the cornfield.

That meant the NanoCam was somewhere in this room.

If only I could see it! Zac thought.

The professor was holding what looked like a little remote control. He tapped at the remote with his thumb. Glancing back up at the screen on the wall, Zac saw the camera view pan around until it was pointed squarely at his face.

So that's what he's using to steer the NanoCam.

'I must say, you made quite an entrance!' said Professor Voler, in the tone of an old man talking to his favourite grandson. 'And you're safely here now. Come and sit down, have some tea.'

'What did you say?' said Zac.

'Some tea, boy!' said Professor Voler, reaching for an ancient-looking teapot. As he did so, Zac noticed that Voler was wearing a strange, fingerless, silver glove. It had a small glassy bubble set into the palm.

The professor poured out two cups of hot, brown liquid and pushed one of them across the table in Zac's direction.

Whatever Zac had expected from Professor Voler, a hot drink had not been on the list.

'It *is* tea, Zachary,' said Voler, reading Zac's expression. 'I'm not trying to poison you. Go ahead and scan it if you'd like.'

Zac whipped out his SpyPad and scanned the tea cup. The reading came up almost instantly.

Contents:
English
Breakfast tea
Temperature: 81°C
Toxins: None

'You see?' said Professor Voler. 'Now then, have a seat.'

'No,' said Zac.

'Come now, Zachary,' said Voler sternly.

'There's no need for that tone. What time is it?'

Zac checked his watch.

'A few minutes shy of midday, correct?' said Voler. 'And as you're aware, I don't plan to break into the GIB vault until 9:00am tomorrow. Surely there's time for a spot of tea before we get down to business?'

Zac had no idea what to make of Professor Voler.

He had been expecting another crazy evil genius in a lab coat who would try to tie him up, or throw him behind a force field. Zac could handle bad guys like that.

But here was Professor Voler, a kindly old man, sitting calmly in his chair, offering him a cup of tea.

'Professor Voler,' Zac said firmly, trying to get this mission back on track. 'Please put the teapot down and step away from the table.'

'Come now,' said Voler, 'is this really necessary? After all, I've welcomed you into my home and –'

'I only came here to get back what you stole!' Zac retorted.

'Of course,' said Voler. 'But obviously I can't let you do that.'

'Let me?' said Zac, staring at the skinny old man. 'No offense, but you're not exactly going to put up much of a fight, are you?'

'Oh no,' Voler replied, shaking his head. 'I can't stand violence. Too messy.'

'Then what do you...'

Zac's SpyPad beeped suddenly, cutting him short. It was Leon. Zac reached down to answer the call.

FLASH!

A bright light flared suddenly in Voler's left palm. The SpyPad slipped from Zac's grasp and flew across the table.

'I'm sorry, Zachary,' said the professor,

catching the SpyPad in his gloved hand and tossing it aside. 'But it really is very poor manners to answer your phone at the tea table.'

Zac's eyes were fixed on Voler's glove.

Suddenly, the professor seemed a whole lot less friendly.

CHAPTER... ...SIX

'Impressive, isn't it?' said Professor Voler, flexing his hand. 'Magnetic Field Gloves. I picked up a pair of them from a weapons designer in Nigeria.'

Zac glared at the professor. 'Picked them up?' he said. 'Stole them, you mean.'

'Well, yes, I suppose that's one way of looking at it,' Voler said with a nod.

'Like you stole the NanoCam,' Zac continued, taking a step towards the professor. 'Like you stole *all* of this stuff! You sit there acting all polite and friendly with your cups of tea and you think you're this big shot treasure hunter, but you're not! You're just a thief!'

'Zachary Power,' said Voler in his slow, calm voice, 'I will not tolerate such rudeness from guests in my home. Please calm down and drink your tea like a –'

'No,' said Zac.

Professor Voler pulled out what looked like a mobile phone, pushed a button and said, 'Alistair, may I see you in the lounge?'

A door hissed open behind Voler and

an enormous man stepped into the room.

'Alistair,' said Voler, 'Our guest is becoming difficult. Would you kindly teach him some manners?'

Alistair cracked his knuckles and nodded.

'I thought you said you couldn't stand violence!' said Zac as the man began moving towards him.

'I can't,' said Voler. 'Fortunately for me, *he* can.'

Zac turned and bolted out of the room. Bravery was one thing, but this guy could have snapped him in half with two fingers.

Other than the door Alistair had just come through, there was only one way out of the room. Zac dashed towards the other door and raced through it.

Slamming the door shut behind him and flipping the lock, Zac turned to find himself inside the jet's cockpit.

For a few seconds, Zac thought he had just found an easy way out of this mission. He could just take the controls and land the jet himself!

But a quick glance at the dashboard told him that everything was locked down and password protected.

Why can it never be that easy? he thought, looking for another way out.

A loud thud echoed from behind the cockpit door. Zac knew it wouldn't be long before Alistair broke the door down.

Zac looked at his watch.

Time to find another way out of here, he thought. *Maybe there's a —*

But then Zac caught sight of something that distracted him completely.

Sitting on top of a control panel, bobbing up and down in a jar of clear liquid, was a pair of *eyeballs.*

Zac's stomach lurched horribly.

What in the world was Voler doing with someone else's —

SHUNK!

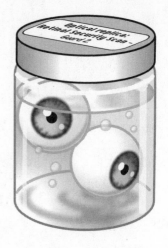

Zac spun around. The cockpit door had just slid open a few centimetres and then stuck again.

'Almost there, sir,' said a gravelly voice from the room outside.

'Not to worry, Alistair,' said Voler calmly. 'He's got nowhere to go.'

But at that moment, Zac saw that there *was* somewhere for him to go.

Set into the floor of the cockpit was an air vent.

It looked just about big enough for him to squeeze into.

Zac lifted up the air vent, revealing a dusty little tunnel. He stuck his head inside and started crawling.

SHUNK!

The cockpit door had moved again.

Far enough for Alistair to fit through? Zac wondered.

Breathing in, he squeezed his way further into the narrow tunnel, but his legs were still sticking out into the cockpit.

SHHHUNK!

Zac commando-crawled further into the tunnel. He was almost there! If he could just…

Suddenly, Zac felt a huge hand wrap around his ankle.

'Not so fast, Zac,' Alistair grumbled. 'You and I need to have a little chat.'

CHAPTER
SEVEN

With one enormous tug, Alistair wrenched Zac clear of the tunnel and tossed him up over his shoulder.

Zac tried to fight back, but the enormous man hardly seemed to notice.

Alistair carried Zac back across Voler's lounge room, through the doorway at the other end, and into a tiny room like a prison cell. It was empty except for a little wooden chair.

Zac landed with a thud as Alistair dropped him onto the floor in the corner of the room.

'Hand me your parachute,' said Alistair gruffly, holding out his hand.

'What parachute?' said Zac, playing dumb.

'Your brother handed you a small parachute just before you took off,' said Alistair matter-of-factly.

Zac realised that he had seen all this from the NanoCam.

'It's sitting in your left pocket,' Alistair added. 'Take it out and hand it to me.'

GIB MICRO-CHUTE – POCKET AIR SAFETY DEVICE

Zac pulled the Micro-Chute from his pocket and handed it to Alistair, who promptly ripped it in half like it was a piece of paper.

'Thank you,' Alistair said. Then he turned and walked out of the cell, shutting the door behind him.

A moment later...

HISSSSSSSSSS...

Zac looked around, searching for the source of the noise.

A stream of dark grey smoke was pouring steadily from a little black box on the roof of the cell.

That might be a sedative, thought Zac. *Knock-out gas.*

Seconds ticked by, and the smoke wafted lower and lower.

Zac ripped off his shirt, scrunched it up, and held it over his mouth and nose, trying to avoid breathing in the gas.

He searched desperately for another exit, but the only way out was through the doorway that Alistair was guarding. Zac could see the professor's bodyguard staring coldly back at him from behind the little glass window set into the door.

By now, the smoke was seeping through Zac's balled-up shirt, and he began to feel light-headed.

Zac's legs grew shaky underneath him and he lost his balance.

He tripped over, asleep before he'd even collapsed on the cold metal floor.

Zac groaned and slowly opened his eyes. As his vision began to clear, he realised that he was still lying on the floor of the little cell.

The smoke had gone now and looking up, Zac saw that Alistair was no longer standing guard outside.

He pushed himself up and glanced down at his watch.

No! How could he possibly have been asleep for that long?

Professor Voler was going to break into the GIB vault in less than an hour!

Zac racked his brains for a way out of

this cell, but his head was still a little hazy from the effects of the smoke.

He closed his eyes, trying to get his brain to start running at full speed again. He was usually so good at getting himself out of sticky situations, but... *That's it!*

An escape plan had suddenly dropped into Zac's head. He walked across the room and started hammering on the door.

'Hey!' he shouted. 'Hey, come here!'

After a few moments, Alistair's face reappeared on the other side of the glass. He motioned for Zac to sit back down in the corner of the cell, then opened the door and stepped inside.

The bodyguard sat down on the little wooden chair.

Zac was surprised that the whole thing didn't just shatter into toothpicks under his enormous bum.

'What do you want?' said Alistair.

'I've made a decision,' said Zac.

'Oh?' said Alistair. 'What might that be?'

'I've decided there's no way I can overpower you,' said Zac.

'Yeah, no kidding,' the giant grinned, leaning back lazily on the chair.

'And if I can't fight back or escape,' said Zac, slowly shifting his feet, 'then I might as well start doing what Professor Voler wants. I'm better off spending my time drinking tea out there rather than freezing my bum off on this cold floor, right?'

'You're smarter than I thought, kid,' said Alistair, tipping back even further on his chair. 'The professor is a brilliant man. One day you'll...'

Zac sprung forward in a flash and launched his full weight into Alistair's stomach.

Caught off-guard, Alistair fell backwards and landed with a thud on the floor.

'Didn't your teacher ever tell you not to lean back on your chair?' said Zac, standing up and pulling out the little black towel that Leon had given him.

Zac held the towel over Alistair's head and squeezed it as hard as he could with both hands.

The yellow goo that Zac had mopped up earlier poured out of the towel in a huge stream, splashing across Alistair's face.

While Alistair struggled against the goo, Zac dashed through the doorway.

Then he slammed his hand down on the locking mechanism, sealing the giant inside.

To the right of the door was a small black button marked SEDATIVE.

Zac hit the button and shook his head at Alistair as fresh clouds of grey smoke filled the cell.

'Oldest trick in the book, Alistair.'

CHAPTER... EIGHT

Zac tore back up the hallway.

He was just about to burst back into Voler's lounge room when he noticed something moving around inside.

Rolling up and down the lounge room, like a guard dog on patrol, was a round, black object. It was about the size of a soccer ball and looked like it was made out of metal.

Zac stopped at the doorway and watched the robotic ball. It was probably harmless, but just in case, he pulled off one of his shoes and tossed it into the room.

PEOOWW! PEOOWW!

Two blue lasers erupted from the metal ball at the first sign of movement. The shoe was a smouldering wreck before it hit the ground.

I guess this means I'm no longer welcome at the tea party, thought Zac, staring at the smoking remains of his shoe.

He needed a way to fool the motion sensor. In the far corner of the room Zac noticed an ancient-looking lounge chair piled high with fluffy cushions.

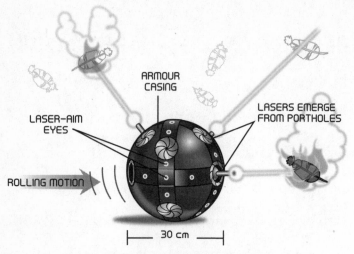

ARMOUR CASING

LASER-AIM EYES

LASERS EMERGE FROM PORTHOLES

ROLLING MOTION

├─── 30 cm ───┤

'VOLER-ROLLER' LASER SECURITY ORB

I wonder...He pulled off his other shoe and hurled it at the lounge.

PEOOWW! PEOOWW!

The twin lasers shot straight through Zac's shoe and into the pile of cushions. The cushions exploded, blasting a giant cloud of white feathers into the air.

And just as Zac had hoped…

PEOOWW PEOOWW PEOOWW!!

The metal security ball went nuts, spinning around frantically, trying to shoot down every last one of the feathers. There were hundreds!

The ball spun faster and faster, smoking, sparks flying, firing shot after shot, until…

BLAM!

A plume of black smoke burst out of the ball. It gave one final shudder and rolled over, broken.

Zac stepped cautiously out into the lounge room. Professor Voler was nowhere to be seen.

Zac glanced up at the big screen on the wall, hoping that this would give him a clue about where the NanoCam was.

But rather than a live picture of himself staring down from the screen, Zac now saw the high-tech city of Bladesville stretching out in front of him.

Enormous skyscrapers loomed as the NanoCam zoomed above the city streets towards the GIB high-security vault.

At least this meant Voler had given up watching Zac's every move. But now the NanoCam was outside the jet, and out of reach. *Which means that I need to get hold of Professor Voler's remote,* thought Zac, *and disable the camera from in here.*

He checked the time.

Nineteen minutes until Voler gets into the vault!

Ducking around behind the tea table, Zac found his SpyPad and stuck it back into his pocket.

He looked over at the doorway into the cockpit. It was shut tight again. That had to be where the professor had gone.

But it was no good just rushing in there without a plan. For all Zac knew, there could be ten more bodyguards as big as Alistair waiting for him.

Something bright and shimmering suddenly caught Zac's eye.

Sitting neatly folded on a shelf was a pair of the most disgusting-looking pants Zac had ever seen. They were bright pink and covered in horrible gold flowers.

A small label was stitched into the back:

PARACHUTE PANTS
G.A.D.G.E.T. standard issue
PULL CORD TO ENGAGE CHUTE

A parachute! This could come in really handy if he needed to make a quick getaway. But if anyone *saw* him in these gross old hippy pants…

Zac rolled his eyes. *Come on,* he told himself, *time to be a professional.*

With a sigh, Zac picked up the big, baggy pants and slipped them on over his jeans. *Great,* he thought. *I look like a boy band drop-out.*

Zac continued searching. He still needed something to help him get hold of that remote. *Aha!*

Sitting on the next shelf across was a fingerless glove just like the one Voler had used to steal Zac's SpyPad.

Zac picked it up and slipped it onto his right hand.

Glancing back up at the plasma screen on the wall, Zac realised with a start that the NanoCam was no longer flying above the streets of Bladesville. It was zooming around inside a big, dark room.

Barely visible in the darkness was row after row of neatly stacked containers, each one stamped with the same logo: *Government Investigation Bureau.*

The NanoCam was *inside* the GIB vault.

CHAPTER... NINE

There was no time to waste.

Baggy parachute pants swishing loudly as he ran, Zac dashed across to the cockpit and opened the door. He was careful to hide his gloved hand behind his back.

Looking out the front window, Zac saw that the jet had now come to a stop, hovering high above the enormous city.

And there was Professor Voler, sitting in the black leather pilot's chair, gazing calmly out at the city. He held the NanoCam remote in his hand.

The professor turned in his chair as Zac took a step forwards. He looked down at Zac's flowery pants and gave a small smile.

For a moment, neither of them spoke.

'I don't get it,' said Zac, breaking the silence. 'How is the NanoCam going to help you break into the GIB vault anyway? It's just a camera!'

'It's already helped me immensely,' said Voler. 'As I'm sure you saw, the camera is small enough to squeeze under the door of the vault, so I've been able to have a good poke around and decide which items to take for my collection.'

'But that still doesn't get you inside,' said Zac.

'No,' said Voler. 'But these will.'

Professor Voler held up the jar that Zac had seen earlier. He reached in and pulled out the two eyeballs, rolling them around in his hand.

'Access to the GIB vault is protected by a retinal scanner,' Voler explained. 'Any person who wishes to enter the vault must first have their eyes scanned to prove they are permitted to go inside.'

'So you *stole* somebody's *eyes*?' said Zac, disgusted.

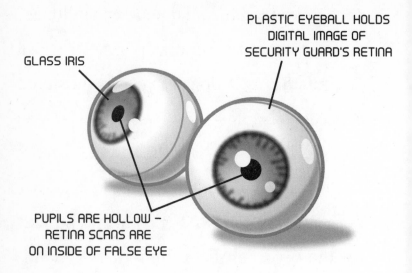

PLASTIC EYEBALL HOLDS
DIGITAL IMAGE OF
SECURITY GUARD'S RETINA

GLASS IRIS

PUPILS ARE HOLLOW –
RETINA SCANS ARE
ON INSIDE OF FALSE EYE

Voler burst out laughing. 'Gracious, is
that what you thought? No, boy, these eyes
are artificial replicas of the security guard
in charge of the vault. I had them created
using photos taken by the NanoCam.'

'So, what, you just hold them up to the
scanner?' Zac asked.

Voler chuckled. 'Something like that.'

This was crazy. Zac didn't care if those things *were* fake. Any person who carried someone else's eyeballs around in a jar was just plain twisted.

'Where is Alistair?' the professor asked, as though he had just noticed that his bodyguard wasn't there.

'Back there in that cell,' said Zac, trying not to sound too proud of himself. 'Out for the count.'

'Is he really?' said Voler. 'Goodness, you did well to overpower him. There aren't many who could do that.'

'Yeah,' said Zac. 'So just imagine what I could do to you.'

'You wouldn't harm an old man sitting in his chair?' Voler asked.

'No,' said Zac firmly. 'But I will take your remote.'

Zac stretched out his gloved right hand towards Professor Voler. He tensed his fingers, and the glassy bubble in his palm flashed to life.

The NanoCam remote flew through the air towards Zac. But before he could grab hold of it, Professor Voler leapt to his feet, and held out his own gloved hand in front of him.

The remote stopped dead in mid-air, caught between the two magnetic fields that were pulling it in opposite directions.

Zac strained his arm backwards against the magnetic attraction, but Voler was surprisingly strong for an old man.

For a full minute they stood there, both pulling with all their might. But the remote still quivered in the air between them.

Well, thought Zac, *this is going nowhere fast.*

Still pulling at the remote control with his gloved hand, Zac slipped his other hand into his pocket, pulled out his SpyPad and set it to Laser.

Then Zac waved his SpyPad in Voler's direction, sending the bright red laser beam flashing across his face.

The laser passed over the professor's

eyes and, for a split second, he squinted and turned away.

It was all Zac needed. With one final flick of his wrist, the remote control zoomed into his hand. Zac dropped it to the floor and smashed it to pieces under his heel.

Voler straightened up, looking furious.

'Hand over the eyeballs,' said Zac.

The professor glared at Zac, and then dropped the fake eyeballs on the floor of the cockpit and kicked them across the floor towards him.

'Now,' said Zac, 'here's what you're going to do. You're going to take this jet and land it at the outskirts of the city. Then you're going to deactivate the cloaking device and wait patiently in that chair for the police to arrive.'

'As delightful as that sounds,' said Voler calmly, 'I must decline your offer. I simply cannot stand prison food.'

And before Zac had time to react, Voler bolted past him out of the cockpit.

CHAPTER... ...TEN

Zac thundered after Professor Voler, bursting back into the lounge room just in time to see him shoulder the GIB jetpack and disappear through the tunnel in the floor.

Losing no time, Zac dived down after the professor. He crashed down into the cargo hold and leapt to his feet again.

'I'd stay back if I were you,' the professor warned. He raised his foot high in the air and brought it down hard against the cargo hold's door.

CLANG!

The door flew off its hinges, tumbling down to earth.

Professor Voler turned towards the open hatch, pulling the jetpack's straps tight around his shoulders.

'Wait!' called Zac. 'There's not enough fuel!'

But it was too late. Voler had already thrown himself out into the open sky.

Without thinking, Zac sprinted across and jumped out after Professor Voler.

As Zac fell through the air, he guessed that he had less than two minutes before he got splattered on the footpath. Two minutes to catch Professor Voler and land safely.

Below him, Zac saw the professor fire up the jetpack to slow his fall, unknowingly burning up the last of his fuel.

Still free-falling, Zac was now plummeting to earth much more quickly than Voler.

Within seconds, he had closed the gap between the two of them.

Zac crashed down on top of the professor and grabbed onto his shoulders.

The impact sent the jetpack spiralling

out of control. Zac held fast to Voler, and the pair of them spun wildly around in a circle.

Zac twisted in mid-air, struggling to keep hold of Professor Voler. At the same time he was trying to avoid being burnt by the jetpack's exhaust.

'Let...*go!*' grunted the professor, struggling to shake Zac off his back.

The jetpack sputtered and shook as the fuel tanks ran dry.

'Listen!' Zac shouted against the rushing wind. 'You've used up all the fuel! If you don't hold on to me, you'll...'

But with one furious shove, Professor Voler broke free from Zac's grasp.

Zac reached out to grab him again, but it was no use. The professor was tumbling wildly towards the ground.

Zac had no choice. He pulled on the ripcord at his waist and activated the parachute pants.

The seat of Zac's pants suddenly billowed up and he slowed to a drift, his body hanging upside-down.

Unfortunately, this made it look like Zac's bum had been inflated to a hundred times its normal size.

Zac sighed. *Not exactly my most glamorous spy moment.*

It took several minutes for Zac to make his way to the ground. Finally he touched

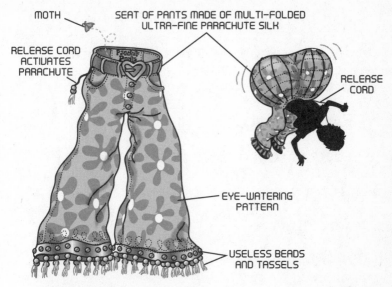

MOTH

SEAT OF PANTS MADE OF MULTI-FOLDED
ULTRA-FINE PARACHUTE SILK

RELEASE CORD
ACTIVATES
PARACHUTE

RELEASE
CORD

EYE-WATERING
PATTERN

USELESS BEADS
AND TASSELS

PARACHUTE PANTS (G.I.B 1969 G.A.D.G.E.T. STANDARD ISSUE)

down in a deserted alley, landing lightly on all fours. He stood up, pulled the cord again, and the pants shrank back to normal.

Zac made his way out of the alley and into a busy Bladesville street.

People passing by stopped and stared at him. He couldn't really blame them. He was shoeless and wearing really ugly parachute pants.

Zac gazed up and down the street, searching for some sign of Professor Voler.

He hated to think what he might find. After a fall like that, all that would be left of the professor would be…

'No way!' Zac whispered.

Smeared across the footpath up ahead of him was a large puddle of something yellow and sticky.

Voler must have used the jetpack's cushioning gel to soften his fall! Zac doubted whether even Leon would have expected the goo to work *that* well.

Zac's SpyPad beeped suddenly. It was Agent Shadow.

'Agent Rock Star,' she said, raising an eyebrow at his bizarre outfit. 'We tracked your landing on WorldEye. Mission accomplished?'

'Mostly,' said Zac. 'Voler got away, but the NanoCam is safe inside the vault. And somewhere in the sky, there's a massive jet filled with stolen technology just waiting to be hauled back to HQ.'

'Excellent work, Agent Rock Star!' Shadow replied.

'Thanks,' said Zac.

'Oh, I nearly forgot,' Agent Shadow said. 'Your brother has asked me to inform you that he has decided to retire as undefeated pool champion of the family.'

It was clear from her confused expression that she had no idea what this message meant.

'He wishes to remind you,' Agent Shadow continued, 'That this means you have some vacuuming to do – *the hard way*.'

...THE END...

MISSION CHECKLIST
How many have you read?

- POISON ISLAND 1
- DEEP WATERS 2
- MIND GAMES 3
- FROZEN FEAR 4
- TOMB OF DOOM 5
- NIGHT RAID 6
- LUNAR STRIKE 7
- SUDDEN DROP 8
- BLOCKBUSTER 9
- SHOCKWAVE 10
- HIGH RISK 11
- UNDERCOVER 12
- SKY HIGH 13
- VOLCANIC PANIC 14
- BOOT CAMP 15
- SWAMP RACE 16
- HORROR HOUSE 17
- THRILL RIDE 18
- CLOSE SHAVE 19
- SHIPWRECK 20